Santa's Littlest Helper Travels the World

Typeset in Monotype Garamond
Art created with acrylics on cardboard

Published by Bloomsbury U.S.A. Children's Books
175 Fifth Avenue, New York, NY 10010
Distributed to the trade by Holtzbrinck Publishers

Library of Congress Cataloging-in-Publication Data
Stohner, Anu.
[Kleine Weihnachtsmann reist um die Welt. English]
Santa's Littlest Helper travels the world / by Anu Stohner ; illustrations by Henrike Wilson. — 1st U.S. ed.
p.   cm.
"Translation . . . by Bloomsbury Publishing PLC"—Copyright p.
Summary: When almost all of Santa's helpers come down with Christmas pox just before the holiday,
the Littlest Helper comes up with a plan to get all the presents delivered in time.
ISBN-13: 978-1-59990-187-9 • ISBN-10: 1-59990-187-0
[1. Christmas—Fiction. 2. Elves—Fiction. 3. Size—Fiction. 4. Animals—Fiction.
5. Voyages and travels—Fiction.] I. Wilson, Henrike, ill. II. Bloomsbury (Firm). III. Title.
PZ7.S8699Sanw 2007   [E]—dc22   2007012009

First U.S. Edition 2007
Printed in China
1 3 5 7 9 10 8 6 4 2

Santa's Littlest Helper Travels the World

Anu Stohner * Henrike Wilson

BLOOMSBURY
CHILDREN'S
BOOKS

In a little village far, far to the north, Santa and his Helpers were very, very busy – just like every year. They were wrapping presents, baking treats, polishing the sleighs and grooming the reindeer. It was a hive of activity!

But one of Santa's Helpers had started preparing long before the others. He had finished packing his sleigh and even had enough time to build a big snowman. He was, of course, Santa's Littlest Helper!

The other Helpers moaned
because they still had so much
to do.

"We've only three more
days to go! Can't you give
us a hand?" they asked the
Littlest Helper.

"Why should I?" he teased.

"It's all right for some!"
said the other Helpers.

The Littlest Helper chuckled and then happily joined in loading the sleighs anyway. Every year they helped Santa deliver presents to children around the world – everyone except for Santa's Littlest Helper. He had the special job of delivering presents to all the animals.

When Christmas Eve finally arrived,
the Littlest Helper woke up very early,
excited about the big journey that lay ahead.
He opened the door of his cottage and looked
down the hill to the village. The village was in
complete darkness, except for one building where
all the windows glowed with light – the hospital.
The Littlest Helper thought something must be wrong.
He put on his skis and headed down the hill.

The Littlest Helper peered
carefully into the large hospital
ward. It was a disaster! All of Santa's
Helpers were lying in bed, covered in
red spots!

"It's the Christmas pox!" declared the doctor.

"Is it contagious?" asked the Chief Helper.

"Very!" replied the doctor.

"Uh-oh!" gasped the Littlest Helper from his hiding place.

The doctor and Chief Helper quickly turned around and
shooed him away. They looked worried.

It would be impossible for the Chief Helper and the Littlest Helper to visit all the children alone. And the doctor must stay back and look after his patients. But the Littlest Helper had an idea.

"I've got it! Let's ask the animals to help!" he said to the Chief Helper.

"The animals?" said the Chief Helper. "Of course, what a wonderful idea! But you will have to ask them, since they'll listen only to you."

As soon as the animals heard what had happened, they wanted to help.
And just like every year, the great journey began – but with a little difference . . .
As Santa, Chief Helper, bear, fox and all the other animals took the reins of
their sleighs, they set off across the great blanket of ice in the north – past
mountains, valleys and rivers towards the biggest cities and the smallest villages.
And the Littlest Helper was in the lead!

In one city the buildings were so tall that the owl felt light-headed, but she didn't let it show. Only the city mouse she was carrying on her back thought he noticed a teeny-weeny tremble.

In the next city stood a huge tower made completely of iron. Elk wanted to know what it was for.

"For absolutely nothing – it's just beautiful," said the clever fox.

"Just like the antlers on his head," giggled the field mouse, but luckily the elk couldn't hear him.

Another city was built in the sea, and the streets were made of big and small canals instead of roads.

"Hopefully no one will fall in the water!" said the Chief Helper.

"Have no fear," grumbled the bear, "we can swim."

The rabbit said nothing, and only the Littlest Helper saw how nervously he scratched one of his long ears with his back paw.

Only once did the Littlest Helper
get carried away with the excitement.
He went under a bridge rather than
flying over the top, as it ought to be
done. But the Chief Helper didn't
mind too much – not tonight!

Through the long night they flew without rest.
When dawn slowly crept over the horizon, the Chief
Helper climbed stiffly from his sleigh. He thought quietly
to himself that he was a little old for such adventures. Next
year he would make sure the Helpers got their shots, and then
maybe he could stay at home and drink apple cider.

Back home around the fire, Herbert
settled into his armchair with a mug
of apple cider. He thanked the
stars for his brilliant idea
and for all his hard work.

Santa's Littlest Helper drank hot blueberry juice,
and there were as many Christmas treats as he
could possibly hope to eat! Now, finally, it was
time for the animals to receive their presents.
Everyone had a wonderful time, and only
the badger missed out – he was so tired,
he fell asleep before the presents
were unwrapped.

Unfortunately, back in the hospital, the sick Helpers got only a little soup and medicine.

"At least another week in bed," said the doctor sternly.

"Can't we have gingerbread?" they asked. "It's supposed to be good for you."

"Not for Christmas pox," said the doctor – and he would know.
   They grumbled a bit, but they comforted themselves with the thought of New Year's punch!

And the children? They were overjoyed with their presents
and didn't even notice the unusual Helpers on Christmas Eve.
Only one little boy, named Jack, had woken up and secretly
peeped out of his window. Since then he has tried to tell
his friends that Santa Claus looks a little bit like an elk.
But of course no one believes him!